THE AMERICAN GIRLS

1764 KAYA, an adventurous Nez Perce girl whose deep love for horses and respect for nature nourish her spirit

1774 FELICITY, a spunky, spritely colonial girl, full of energy and independence

1824 JOSEFINA, a Hispanic girl whose heart and hopes are as big as the New Mexico sky

1854 KIRSTEN, a pioneer girl of strength and spirit who settles on the frontier

1864 ADDY, a courageous girl determined to be free in the midst of the Civil War

1904 SAMANTHA, a bright Victorian beauty, an orphan raised by her wealthy grandmother

1934 KIT, a clever, resourceful girl facing the Great Depression with spirit and determination

1944 MOLLY, who schemes and dreams on the home front during World War Two

1854

MEET
Kirsten

An American Girl

BY JANET SHAW

ILLUSTRATIONS RENÉE GRAEF

VIGNETTES PAUL LACKNER

★ American Girl™

Published by Pleasant Company Publications
Copyright © 1986, 2000 by American Girl, LLC
For information, address: Book Editor, Pleasant Company Publications,
8400 Fairway Place, P.O. Box 620998, Middleton, WI 53562.

Visit our Web site at **americangirl.com**.

Printed in China.
06 07 08 09 10 11 LEO 61 60 59 58 57 56

PICTURE CREDITS
The following individuals and organizations have generously given
permission to reprint illustrations contained in "Looking Back": p. 55—Collection of the
New York Historical Society, neg. 21443; pp. 56–57—State Historical Society of Wisconsin,
WHi (W6) 3267; *The America Letter* by Jakob Kulles, courtesy of the Emigrant Institute in Växjö,
Sweden; pp. 58–59—Erlander Home Museum, Swedish Historical Society of Rockford, IL;
Emigrants Arriving to Gothenburg by Geskel Saloman, courtesy Emigrant Institute in Växjö,
Sweden. Copied by Gunnar Johansson; H.M. Hayes by Duncan McFarlane, #1953.3950,
© Mystic Seaport, Mystic, CT; *The Emigrants* by Knut Ekwall in collection
of American Scandinavian Foundation. Courtesy Lena Biörck Kaplan;
p. 61—© Collection of the New York Historical Society, neg. 21443.

Library of Congress Cataloging-in-Publication Data

Shaw, Janet Beeler, 1937–
Meet Kirsten, an American girl
(The American girls collection)
Summary: Nine-year-old Kirsten and her family experience many hardships
as they travel from Sweden to the Minnesota frontier in 1854.
[1. Emigration and immigration—Fiction. 2. Frontier and pioneer life—Fiction.]
I. Graef, Renée, ill. II. Title. III. Series.
PZ7.S53423ME 1986 [Fic] 86-60466
ISBN 0-937295-79-5
ISBN 0-937295-01-9 (pbk.)

FOR MY MOTHER,
NADINA FOWLER

TABLE OF CONTENTS

KIRSTEN'S FAMILY

PAPA
*Kirsten's father, who
is sometimes gruff
but always loving*

MAMA
*Kirsten's mother, who
never loses heart*

KIRSTEN
*A nine-year-old
girl who moves with
her family to a new home
on America's frontier
in 1854*

LARS
*Kirsten's fourteen-year-
old brother, who is
almost a man*

PETER
*Kirsten's mischievous
brother, who is
five years old*

MARTA
*Kirsten's best friend
on the long trip
from Sweden
to Minnesota*

ANNA
*Kirsten's seven-
year-old cousin*

LISBETH
*Kirsten's eleven-
year-old cousin*

UNCLE OLAV
*Kirsten's uncle, who
came to America six
years before Kirsten
and her family*

AUNT INGER
*Kirsten's aunt, who
helps the Larsons feel
at home in America*

AMERICA!

"That's America!" Kirsten said happily. She stood at the ship's railing with her friend Marta and pointed to the green strip of land beyond the waves. Over-head, the tall sails creaked in the wind.

Marta shaded her eyes and pressed against the railing as though that would make the *Eagle* sail faster. "I can't wait to walk on land again," she said, and shivered.

Kirsten touched her friend's thin arm. "Are you cold?" she asked. "Let's go sit where the wind isn't so strong." She tucked her rag doll, Sari, into her shawl and walked to a coil of rope that was as high as a barrel. Then she hitched up her skirt and climbed into a space just big enough for two girls to sit knee to knee and forehead to forehead. Marta crawled in after her.

It was warmer here in the coiled rope, but the wind still whistled overhead. Kirsten took her handkerchief from her pocket and made a cape for Sari. Marta's doll wore her apron like a shawl. "Soon we'll be on land again," Marta told her doll. "Don't worry about the wind."

Kirsten pulled a piece of hard, dry bread from her apron pocket and broke it in two. She and Marta fed their dolls before they chewed the bread themselves. "What's the very first thing you want to do in America?" Kirsten asked.

"I want to pick an apple," Marta said dreamily. "There are apples everywhere in America."

"Apples!" When Kirsten said the word she could almost taste the crisp, delicious fruit. "We'll pick cherries, too!" she said.

"And we'll get fresh bread," Marta added. "I think we'll be there by tonight, don't you?"

"Not if it storms again," Kirsten answered. She peered up at the darkening clouds and pulled her shawl more closely around her shoulders. Above

2

her head she saw the sailors crawling into the
rigging to adjust the sails. Then she heard Papa's
voice.

"Kirsten, where are you?" he called.

Kirsten stood and shouted, "Here I am, Papa!"
Strands of blond hair pulled loose from her braids
and whipped across her cheeks when she raised her
head above the ropes.

Papa's black wool jacket flapped like a gull's
wings as he crossed the deck. "There's a storm
coming," Papa said. "It could be dangerous. The
coast is rocky here, and the wind is getting stronger."

Papa lifted Kirsten out of the coiled rope. Then he pulled Marta out, too. "Come below where we'll be safe," he said.

The clouds rolled like water boiling in Mama's black iron pot. The tops of the waves turned white and crashed over the sides of the ship. They dashed onto Kirsten's boots as she scrambled toward the opening into the hold. "Hurry!" Papa said. He held tightly to Kirsten's and Marta's hands.

As Kirsten climbed down the ladder into the hold, her spirits sank. Of course she didn't want to be washed overboard by the waves, but it was awful to stay in this small room below the deck. For more than two months, twenty Swedish families had been cramped together here. Each family shared one or two of the bunks that lined the walls, and everything they owned was stored in large trunks which stood at the ends of the bunks. The air smelled sour now, and it would be worse when people got seasick. No fresh air could come in when the sailors locked the trap-door against the waves. And the hold was dark,

4

even in the middle of the afternoon. Just one oil lantern swung and sputtered over some tables in the middle of the room. Kirsten could barely see Mama, who was lying on her side in the narrow bunk she shared with Kirsten.

"Here you are," Mama said as Kirsten crawled up beside her. "I asked Papa to find you. I don't know where you can hide on such a small ship."

"Marta and I were playing. We could see land before the storm blew up," Kirsten said.

Mama sighed. "I prayed there would be no more storms so I could be strong when we land in America," she said. She had been sick since the first day they came aboard the ship, and storms made her feel worse.

"You'll be strong soon, I'm sure of it. Don't lose heart, Mama," said Kirsten. But now the wind howled like a pack of wolves. The waves beat against the ship's hull, next to Kirsten's head, and the ship tossed as though it might tip over.

Outside there was a loud crash. Mama put her arm over Kirsten's shoulder. "Don't fall off the bunk," she warned. Buckets tumbled over one another, and old Mr. Peterson's trunk skidded across

*The waves beat against the ship's hull, next to Kirsten's head,
and the ship tossed as though it might tip over.*

the wet floor. The lantern swung wildly, then dropped beneath a table.

"Mama, Lars says the coast is full of rocks. Do you think we'll be blown onto them?" Kirsten asked. She could barely hear her own words above the roar of the storm.

"Don't think about the rocks," Mama said. "Let's think about Uncle Olav's letter instead. Do you remember your Uncle Olav?"

Kirsten had heard about Uncle Olav so many times she *thought* she remembered him. "Tell me," she said. She snuggled close to Mama and tried not to think about the howling storm.

"Olav left Sweden six years ago, when you were just three," Mama said. "He thought he could make a better life in America. And last year, he wrote to tell us about his new farm. The land is rich and good there, and he needs our help."

"In Minne-sota," Kirsten said, stumbling over the strange word.

"Yes, in Minnesota," Mama answered. "Now you tell me something."

"Uncle Olav married Aunt Inger in America," Kirsten said. She thought this was the best part of the story. "Aunt Inger came from Sweden, too."

"That's right," said Mama. "Olav said he married a widow with two daughters."

"My cousins, Anna and Lisbeth," Kirsten finished. "We'll be friends, don't you think?"

"Of course," said Mama. "We'll live on the same farm, and they'll be right next door."

The waves still pounded against the ship. In the dark hold, Kirsten hugged Sari's rag body and whispered, "We're almost there. We're almost home." She tried to imagine a farm right next door to her new cousins. She hoped this American home would be just like the one she left in Sweden, with the maple tree by the door.

When the storm finally passed, Kirsten felt like the barn cat she'd once fished out of the well. Her skirt and shawl were wet and stained. Her boots were soaked. But everyone was safe, the sky was clear, and the *Eagle* was sailing toward the green

coast once more. Kirsten watched the seagulls
swoop and dive as she stood on the deck with Mama
and Papa.

"I smell the earth again," Papa's voice boomed.
He held Peter, who was five, on his hip.

Mama smiled at the shore as though she greeted
a friend. She leaned toward Papa, and Kirsten heard
her whisper, "So many times I lost hope that we'd all
make it to America."

"You're a brave woman," Papa answered. "You
have heart. I'm proud of you and our children."

Kirsten's brother Lars, who was always talking
with the sailors, pushed through the crowd just then.
"The sailors say we'll land in New York tomorrow
morning," Lars said.

"That's wonderful!" Mama replied. "We'll have
fresh bread for breakfast, and I'll find a place to wash
our clothes."

"They say we can't leave the ship until the health
inspector lets us," Lars added.

"What's the health inspector?" Kirsten asked.

"He's a doctor who will look at everyone on the
ship. No one who is sick can stay in America," Lars
explained.

9

"But Mama's sick!" Peter cried. He held out his arms, and Mama hugged him.

"Mama has only been seasick," Papa said in his deep voice. "Almost everyone gets seasick on the ocean. The health inspector looks for illnesses like typhoid and cholera. Illnesses that kill people."

"No one on our ship has cholera," Lars said.

"That's right," Papa replied. "You see, Peter, we don't need to worry. Let's see you smile again. Tomorrow we'll be in New York, and then we'll start our journey to Minnesota."

When the *Eagle* finally docked in New York harbor and the health inspector said that they could leave the ship, Lars bounded down the gangplank. Peter scrambled right behind him. Mama and Papa went next, then Kirsten. She held Sari tightly.

Kirsten was bursting to run and turn circles on the grass she saw near the docks. She was surprised when she stepped off the gangplank and the ground seemed to spin around her. In Sweden, it had been steady under her feet. Here in America, it swayed and rolled like the ship she'd just left. She grabbed Papa's hand. "Why am I so dizzy?" she asked.

"We're all used to the rocking of the ship," Papa answered. "Now we have to get used to dry land all over again."

For a minute, Kirsten stood still. Then she turned and looked back at the *Eagle*. When they boarded the small ship, no one had known what to expect. There had been dangerous storms at sea. They had been sick. But at last they had arrived in America.

What will happen now? Kirsten wondered. But she was more curious than afraid. On wobbly legs, she followed Mama and Papa up the path into the park near the dock.

LOST

Kirsten sat under an oak tree with Mama and Peter. She patted down the grass to make a bed for Sari. Although it was only June, the grass here in the park was already as dry as straw. Summer was so hot in America! Three months ago, when they left the farm in Sweden, Kirsten had needed her wool skirt and shawl. Now her clothes were much too heavy. Even without her quilted petticoats she was hot.

Peter lay on his stomach, watching the road. He was on the lookout for Papa and Lars, who had gone to buy tickets for the rest of their journey. Papa promised that later he would take Peter and Kirsten to buy bread and milk. Kirsten couldn't wait. She wanted to explore this new town, New York. But Mama wouldn't let her go by herself. Swedish children could easily get lost here in America, Mama warned.

While Papa was gone, Kirsten watched the New Yorkers stroll by. The women and girls wore flowered dresses with lots of ruffles. The men wore tight trousers and white jackets. Kirsten looked down at her own tattered clothes. The only fine thing she wore was the amber heart her grandmother had given her on the day they said good-bye. "Oh, Mama, I wish we could wear such pretty dresses," Kirsten said. "Only the people from the ships look like this."

"Our clothes are dry and clean. We don't need to be ashamed," Mama answered. Her cheeks were pink again, and now she smiled. "Besides, how could I milk a cow if I wore so many ruffles?"

Peter made a face. He hated to dress up, even for church. Then his frown turned into a grin and he jumped to his feet. "Here come Papa and Lars!" he called.

Lars held a handful of cherries. Papa scooped more fruit from the knapsack slung over his arm. He gave one big handful to Peter and another to Kirsten. Then he knelt beside Mama to share what was left.

"I've never seen such huge black cherries," Mama said.

"Everything in America is big!" Lars announced. "Wait until you see New York."

"And there will be more to see tomorow," Papa added in a hearty voice. "I just bought our tickets for the trip west. We leave in the morning."

"Did you find an honest agent?" Mama asked with a worried frown. "Old Mr. Peterson was cheated of his money by a dishonest agent. I didn't know there were so many thieves in America."

Papa put his hand on her shoulder. "Yes, our agent is a good man. He left Sweden four years ago, and he knows English well. And he helped me change our money at a bank."

Mama still sighed. "It's such a long way to Minnesota," she said.

"But the agent will guide us all the way to the Mississippi River. He says we'll have to travel only a few weeks more," Papa replied. "And now that we're on land, we'll get our strength back quickly." He smiled. "Don't lose heart."

Mama smiled back. "No, I won't lose heart now."

Peter tugged the sleeve of Papa's shirt. "Let's go buy our milk and bread!" he said.

Mama handed Kirsten the milk pitcher. "Stay close to your father," she warned Kirsten and Peter. "Remember, you don't speak English yet."

Papa took Peter's hand as they walked along the wide, crowded street called Broadway. Kirsten skipped beside them. She held the milk pitcher tightly in one arm and Sari in the other.

Kirsten had never seen so many horses, so many wagons, buggies, carts. Men and women filled the sidewalks. Children darted among them. In her small town in Sweden, Kirsten had known everyone she met. Here, everyone was a stranger. These Americans chattered, called, and shouted all around her. Kirsten couldn't understand a single word they said.

She walked with Papa past carts full of onions

and potatoes. Chickens and ducks
fluttered and squawked in their
coops as they waited to be sold.
"Papa," Kirsten begged, "slow
down! I want to look around."

Now there were candy stores, shops that sold
tobacco, candles, tinware, cloth—oh, everything.
"Here's the bread shop," Papa said. Round loaves of
wheat bread were stacked inside the shop window.
Papa carefully counted out two American coins, and
the shopkeeper gave him several rolls. He handed
one to Kirsten and one to Peter. "Now we'll get
milk," he said.

The fresh bread was soft and sweet. Kirsten
tried to eat slowly to make it last. She kept her
eye on Papa's broad shoulders as she walked
down the busy street, munching. She saw women
holding huge baskets heaped with fruit. She
couldn't understand what the women said, but
the red berries in their baskets reminded her of
the delicious cloudberries her grandmother gathered
in Sweden.

Kirsten paused a moment by a gray-headed
berry seller. Then a boy carrying a tray of silvery

fish bumped her. She almost stumbled over a small black boy who polished a man's boots. "Wait, Papa!" she called over the racket of the horses' hooves on cobblestones.

But Papa was gone. Kirsten had lost sight of him in the crowd.

Clutching Sari, Kirsten ran. She squeezed between women with their shopping baskets. "Papa, wait for me!" she called. But she didn't see Papa. Lots of little boys chased through the crowd, but not one of them was Peter.

Maybe Papa and Peter are already at the milk shop, Kirsten thought. *Maybe they're waiting for me to come with the milk pitcher.* She hurried along, looking in each shop window for cheese and barrels of milk.

Where was the milk shop? Was it on the other side of the street? Kirsten climbed around pigs that poked their snouts in the trash of the gutter. Then she dodged in front of a buggy, ran across the street, and headed down the row of shops. She couldn't find the milk shop anywhere. And this side of the street was even more crowded with shoppers. The babble of their voices made her head swim. "Papa!" Kirsten called. Her cry was lost in the noisy street.

"Papa!" Kirsten called.
Her cry was lost in the noisy street.

18

Kirsten tucked her necklace into her collar
and hugged the milk pitcher tightly. Mama had
said there were thieves in New York, a lot of thieves.
They would steal anything. "Papa! Papa!" Kirsten
shouted. Papa was nowhere to be found.

Maybe I should go back to the park, Kirsten said
to herself. *Mama's waiting there.* But now Kirsten
realized she didn't know where the park was, either.
Which way had she come with Papa? How many
corners had they turned?

She asked a woman with a baby in her arms,
"Please, where is the park by the river?" The woman
kept walking as though she hadn't even heard
Kirsten.

"The park?" Kirsten asked a tall boy with black
hair. He said something to his friend, and they
laughed at her.

"Help me!" Kirsten cried out. "Please help me!"
No one even glanced at her. Couldn't anyone in this
big crowd understand that she was lost?

Sun reflected off the cobblestones, and the
smell of garbage made Kirsten dizzy. Her head spun
as though she were seasick on the ship. But this time
she wasn't seasick. She was frightened. What if she

couldn't find Papa? What if she couldn't find the
park and Mama? What would happen to her in this
huge city if she couldn't find her family?

Again, she began to run. She stumbled and
bumped into barrels. When a dog nipped at her
ankles, she didn't stop running. Now she was on
a different part of the street, where rough-looking
men in bloody aprons sold wild game and meat.
Gutted rabbits, squirrels, and deer hung from poles.
Sides of pork dangled from sharp hooks. The buzz
of flies hummed in her ears.

She headed back the other way, but she
seemed to have turned onto a different street. The
houses were all crowded together, and there were
no shops at all. Papa would never look for her here!
And every turn she took might lead her farther
away from the park where Mama waited.

Kirsten wanted to be brave. She wanted to
have heart, like Mama. But she sank down on the
steps of a brown house, hid her face in her doll's
skirt, and wept. Tears ran between her fingers and
dropped onto her lap. "Oh, Sari," she cried, "what
if we can't find Mama and Papa? Will they go to
Minnesota without us?"

After what seemed like a long time, Kirsten felt a touch on her shoulder. A brown-haired young woman in a long blue apron stood beside her. When the woman spoke, her voice was gentle. She seemed to want to know what was wrong.

"I'm lost!" Kirsten said. The woman didn't understand. She looked puzzled and shook her head, and more tears ran down Kirsten's cheeks.

The woman spoke again. Now she made a motion as if she were pouring. Did she want the milk pitcher? Kirsten clutched it to her chest, and the woman went back inside the house.

"Sari, what will we do!" Kirsten sobbed.

Then the woman was back. This time she held out a tin cup of water. Gratefully, Kirsten drank until there wasn't a drop left. "*Tack!*" she said.

The woman smiled and sat down on the step. She understood "thank you." But how could Kirsten tell her about Papa and the milk shop, and the park near the ship where Mama was waiting? How could they understand each other if their words didn't match? Hopelessly, Kirsten traced the dust at her feet with her fingertip.

Then she had an idea. If she couldn't talk, maybe a picture could talk for her. Carefully, Kirsten outlined the shape of the *Eagle* in the dust. Then she drew two big sails over the ship. She pulled at the corner of the woman's apron and pointed to her drawing.

The woman smiled when she saw the picture.

Quickly, she locked her door, put the key in her apron pocket, and motioned for Kirsten to follow her. At the end of the street, they turned into a smaller lane. After a few more turns, they were beside the

22

river, where the ships were docked.

Far ahead, Kirsten could see the tall oak trees
of Battery Park. And there was the *Eagle*, tied to the
dock. Kirsten ran. She saw the path leading into the
park. And at the top of the path, she saw Mama
and Papa!

"Mama! Papa! Here I am!" Kirsten shouted.

Mama turned and shaded her eyes to look. Papa
began to run down the path, his boots scattering
gravel. Kirsten flung herself first into Papa's arms,
then into Mama's.

"Kirsten, you frightened us!" Papa said. "We
couldn't find you anywhere!"

"I thought you would leave New York without
me," Kirsten whispered against Mama's neck.
Mama's shoulder smelled wonderfully of soap and
dry grass. The sun made her hair look like gold.

"What?" Mama said. "We would never, never
leave you! But how did you find your way back?"

Kirsten realized that the kind woman was gone.
She pointed to her, walking away along the path
beside the river. "I drew a picture of our ship and
that American lady helped me find it."

Papa hugged Kirsten again. "You're a very

smart girl," he told her. "Be smart enough to stay right beside me the next time. Promise?"

"I promise!" Kirsten said, and meant it with all her heart.

ACROSS THE
NEW LAND

The next day Kirsten and her family started the long journey across the country to Minnesota. Not even Papa could guess how long the trip would take. "The agent will help us find our way, and we'll see what happens," he said.

At the top of the path into the park, Kirsten met Marta. "We're leaving today," Kirsten said. "Are you going, too?"

Marta shook her head. "Not until tomorrow," she replied.

"Oh, no! I was so sure we'd be traveling together!" exclaimed Kirsten.

"Me, too," Marta answered softly. "Are you

going to take another ship now, Kirsten?"

"No, I think we're going to take a train," Kirsten said. "What do you think a train looks like, Marta?"

"I don't know exactly. My father says it will make a loud noise and a lot of smoke. We might be afraid of trains," Marta said.

Kirsten grinned. "Noise won't hurt us!" she said. "And Papa says a train is like many wagons all traveling together. Maybe you'll get on our train tomorrow. Wouldn't that be lucky?"

Marta caught her lower lip between her teeth. "Or maybe we won't ever see each other again," she said.

Kirsten took her friend's hand. "But your family is going to Minnesota, just like mine is. We're sure to meet on the way. At least, I hope so," she added.

"I'll miss you, Kirsten," Marta murmured.

Kirsten looked down at her dusty boots. Saying good-bye to the people she loved was the hardest thing in the world to do. She didn't want Marta to see the tears that stung her eyes. So she took a deep breath before she said, "Marta, I'll tell you what my grandmother said to me when we left Sweden.

Mormor said, 'When you're lonely, look at the sun. Remember that we all see the same sun.'"

"Do you do that?" Marta asked. "Do you look at the sun and think of your grandmother?"

"When I miss Mormor, I look at the sun and pray for her," Kirsten said.

Now Marta managed a small smile. "Then when I miss you, I'll look at the sun. Will you do the same?"

"Yes. And say a prayer. I will. I'll say, 'God bless Marta.'"

"I'll say a prayer, too," Marta agreed. "And I'll be looking for you everywhere."

Kirsten sighed. She was going to another new place. It seemed to her she would always feel like a Swedish girl who was far from home. Home—that's a place where you're happy, a place where you belong. *How can America ever really be my home?* she thought. Then she followed her parents down the path to meet the agent and ten new families.

First there was a fierce roar and a hiss, then the long scream of a whistle. Kirsten's heart flip-flopped. Maybe Marta was right to be afraid of trains. The engine looked like a black iron house on fire. Smoke boiled up from the giant smokestack. Live sparks and red coals showered down with the smoke. Kirsten stayed close to Mama. But Mama was worried, too. She squeezed Kirsten's hand extra hard as they climbed aboard.

Inside, the train was so hot it felt ready to explode. There was coal grit on the floor and cinders in the air. Kirsten could hardly get her breath. She saw that the windows had been nailed shut. The agent said the train would be safer this way.

Papa and Lars stood near the door. Kirsten was squeezed beside Mama and Peter on a bench under the windows. Trunks and bundles were piled up in front of them. Kirsten was used to being crowded, but now she felt as if she were packed up inside their big painted trunk.

"Aren't we there yet?" Peter complained.

"Hush, we haven't even started to move," Mama said.

Some of the old folks closed their eyes, and Kirsten knew they were praying that the train wouldn't catch on fire. Then it began to move. It bumped and lurched and screeched over the metal rails. Peter hid his face in Mama's lap. The men were quiet, and even Lars's eyes were wide. The train began to huff and chug. Through the small window, Kirsten saw houses and trees moving backward. The huffing and chugging grew louder, and the trees went by very quickly. Lars called out, "We're going faster than a horse can run! Faster than the fastest horse can run!" Dizzy, Kirsten closed her eyes. The train groaned and swayed. Even though she couldn't see, she felt the speed with which it carried them west.

For days, the train traveled through fields and forests. When they stopped for water, a man from the railroad opened the door for a few minutes, but the air stayed hot and hard to breathe. Everyone was quiet, dazed by the heat. Now and then Mama opened the food trunk, but not even Lars was very hungry. When Kirsten caught his eye, he gave her a sad smile. She knew he hated to be trapped inside even more than she did.

At last they reached Chicago. A hot strong wind blew dirt up from the streets, but Kirsten didn't care how dirty it was. Here she could walk again, and run! Papa said that in a few days they would join a big group of pioneers traveling to the Mississippi River in wagons. But first they would rest here, in a boarding house.

It was good to be in a house again, although this boarding house reminded Kirsten of their big barn in Sweden. The long, open sleeping room upstairs was like the loft where Papa stored hay, except it was filled with row after row of beds and crowded with people's belongings. In the kitchen there were big tubs for Mama to wash their clothes in. When the laundry was finished, Mama sent Kirsten and Peter out into the back yard to get some sun. Kirsten found herself on a long porch filled with children. She was used to smiling at other girls, wishing she spoke their language so that they could talk to each other. But now she

"You're here! You're here!"
Kirsten repeated over and over.

heard someone call her name: "Kirsten Larson!"

It was Marta! Her thick braid swinging, she ran from between the rows of shirts and underwear drying on the clotheslines. She grabbed Kirsten's shoulders, Kirsten grabbed Marta's waist, and they whirled and whirled.

"You're here! You're here!" Kirsten repeated over and over.

"So are you!" Marta answered, again and again.

That evening, Marta's family sat down with Kirsten's family for roast pork and potatoes. Marta's father said, "We're back with our friends again. We'll stay together now until we get to Minnesota." Under the table Kirsten and Marta held hands. Kirsten couldn't believe her good luck. At last America was beginning to feel like home—with good food, a real bed to sleep in, and best of all, friends.

CHAPTER
FOUR
—

A SAD
JOURNEY

Kirsten liked the Mississippi riverboat
the moment she saw it. It was white,
with a pair of wings painted in bright
red on the sides. The boat was named *The Redwing*,
like the red-winged blackbirds that called to one
another along the riverbank. *The Redwing* had broad
decks and a big paddle wheel.

Right away Kirsten wanted to run upstairs to
the wide upper deck. She grabbed Marta's hand,
ducked under a rope, and skipped up the steps. But
before they were to the top step a sailor stopped
them. They didn't understand his words, but they
knew his gesture meant "Get down!"

That evening as they ate their meal of dried

pork and bread, Kirsten asked Papa, "Why can't we go up on the big deck? No one is out there."

"That deck is for rich people," Papa said.

"If we paid more money could we go up there?" asked Kirsten.

Papa rubbed his forehead. "We only have a little money left, Kirsten. And when we leave this boat we'll still have to hire a wagon to reach Olav's farm."

"You've managed our money well," Mama said to Papa. To Kirsten she said crossly, "Don't ask for so much!"

Kirsten was surprised. Mama never talked harshly to her. Why was she cross now? Their long trip was almost over. In a few days they would be at Uncle Olav's.

Kirsten looked closely at her mother. "What's wrong, Mama?" she asked.

Mama said softly, "I'm cross because I'm worried. As we boarded the boat, the sailors were burying a passenger who died of cholera."

"Don't worry so," Lars said to Mama. "We won't get sick! Look at us. We're healthy."

Lars was right. They were strong from walking

beside the wagons on the way to the river and tan from the prairie sun. But Mama didn't smile. "Cholera kills strong ones just like weak ones," she said. "Pray to God that we get safely to Uncle Olav's."

For two days, Kirsten and Marta played together on the riverboat. They watched the hawks circling overhead and counted the fish that jumped from the water. But the third morning, Marta wasn't on the small deck where they were allowed to walk. Marta's father was there alone. He stood at the railing, staring straight ahead at the wide, brown river.

"Where's Marta?" Kirsten asked him.

"Our Marta's very sick," he said. He gripped the railing so tightly that his knuckles were white. "With cholera."

Kirsten's head buzzed. Cholera! Last night after supper, Marta had played with her right here on deck. Last night Marta was perfectly fine. She *couldn't* have cholera now.

"How can she be sick?" Kirsten asked. "She was well yesterday."

"During the night she doubled up with a pain

35

in her belly. Now she aches and moans and burns
with a fever. The captain made us take her to the sick
bay," he said.

"Can I go see her?"

Marta's father took Kirsten's wrist firmly.
"No, Kirsten. You mustn't. You could get sick, too.
Marta's mother is with her. That's all we can do."

But Kirsten had to see Marta. She ran down
below the decks, to the part of the boat called the
sick bay. Marta was there, lying on a straw mat
near the entrance. Her knees were drawn up to her
chest. Her mouth was open as though she couldn't
breathe. When her mother tried to wipe her forehead, Marta trembled and moaned. Her lips were
dry and cracked and her eyelids fluttered.

"Marta," Kirsten whispered. She took a step
toward her friend, but Marta's mother sent her
away. "Go back to your family, Kirsten. It's
dangerous for you here. Marta will get better,
you'll see."

Still, Kirsten stayed near the sick bay until
Mama found her. "I've looked everywhere for you!"
Mama said. "There's nothing we can do for Marta.
Not with cholera. You must take care of yourself,

Kirsten! Stay close to me and Papa, please."

So Kirsten stayed close to Mama, but her thoughts were with her sick friend. She told herself that Marta would get well. Over and over she said, *She must get well!*

Kirsten wasn't able to eat, and that night she was sure she would never sleep. But she fell into a restless doze. Later, she woke up with a start. Something was terribly wrong, but in her sleep she'd forgotten what it could be. Then she remembered Marta.

Kirsten ran down to the sick bay. Through the

parted curtains she saw that Marta was gone. *She's better then*, Kirsten thought. She ran up to the deck to find her friend.

The sun was just rising. The riverboat was anchored at a sandy beach below tall bluffs. A gangplank had been lowered for some sailors, who carried a wooden box on their shoulders. They walked along the shore.

Marta's father stood at the railing where Kirsten had seen him last. His arm was around Marta's mother.

Kirsten grabbed Marta's father's sleeve. "Where's Marta?" she asked.

He pointed to the sailors with their box. "Our Marta died last night, Kirsten. The sailors will bury her here. Her soul is in heaven." Then he hid his face in his hand.

"She can't be dead!" Kirsten cried. "She can't be!" Kirsten felt as though her heart was ripped in two. She heard deep sobs that hardly seemed her own. They filled up her chest. She tried to say her friend's name, but her lips wouldn't form the words.

Then Kirsten felt Mama's arms around her,

Mama cradled her and said softly,
"Let her have her tears."

and Papa patted her shoulder. "Enough crying. Stop now, Kirsten," he said.

But Mama cradled her and said softly, "Let her have her tears."

HOME AT LAST

It was raining when the Larsons left *The Redwing*. Kirsten didn't watch the riverboat pull away from the dock. She didn't ever want to see that boat again, because Marta had died on it. She was lonely for Marta, and there wasn't any sun in Minnesota to look at with a prayer. So Kirsten looked at the town of Riverton. She saw wet houses, wet trees, and wet horses pulling wagons loaded with wet logs. She blinked into the rain. "God bless you, Marta," she whispered.

Mama touched her cheek. "Cheer up, Kirsten! When Papa and the boys come back with a wagon, it will only take a few hours to reach Olav's farm."

But Papa frowned with worry when he strode back to the dock where Kirsten and Mama waited. "We don't have enough money left to rent a horse and wagon," he said.

Mama's shoulders slumped. "What will we do?" she asked.

Papa made his voice strong. "We have our good legs. We'll walk to Olav's farm. We'll just have to leave the trunks here."

Mama looked first at the big painted trunk that held their most precious things, then at the black food trunk with Papa's name lettered on its side. "Everything we own in the world is in these trunks," she said sadly. "How can we get along without our clothes and your tools?"

"We'll take what we can carry now, and we'll have the trunks shipped later," Papa said. "Don't lose heart." He began taking blankets and tools from the big trunk.

After a moment, Mama said, "It can't be helped. We'll send for them soon. People are more important than things, and we're all together and well, thank God." She made a bundle of the bread and cheese that was left, then closed the food trunk.

42

Papa said, "We need everyone's hands today. Kirsten, you must put your doll here with the other things. You can get her again when the trunks are shipped to us."

Kirsten knew she couldn't say no to Papa. Gently, she put Sari on top of the sweaters and linens in the painted trunk. Before Papa closed the top, she kissed Sari's faded cheek. "You'll be with me soon," she whispered. Then Papa fastened the lock, and he and Lars dragged the trunks to the warehouse.

The family followed Papa down the road along

the river, past tiny houses built of split logs. Everyone carried a bundle, and they walked for hours.
Kirsten's boots were heavy with mud. Her wool skirt
was soaked through to her petticoat. Sometimes she
heard a cow moo, but there were long stretches of
forest or prairie between farms. Even Lars was tired
now. He walked with his head down, his long hair
plastered to his neck by the rain.

By afternoon the rain stopped. The sky was a
smooth, blue bowl. Meadowlarks flew up from the
fields, and daisies and black-eyed Susans bloomed
beside the road. The Larsons were a long, long way
from town when they stopped to eat lunch.

"Olav wrote us the truth," Papa said. "The soil
here is good. We'll have a better life." Before they
walked on, Kirsten picked a daisy for Mama to wear
at her collar.

Now Papa asked the way at each farm they
passed. At last he said, "The next one is Olav's!"
In the distance, Kirsten could see a house, a large
barn, and a tiny cabin. Cows ambled
down the field toward the barn to be
milked. Smoke rose from the chimney
of the house.

Lars and Peter began to run, splashing through puddles. Lars shouted, "Hello!" and Peter cried, "We're here! We're here!"

A man with a smile like Papa's came from the barn. Two girls and a woman ran from the house. They waved and called out, "Hello! Hello! It's you! At last!"

Suddenly Kirsten was shy. She shrank back behind Mama. Then she heard her own name above the shouts and laughter. "Kirsten? You must be Kirsten!"

The taller girl, who had brown braids and gray eyes, took the heavy bundle from Kirsten's arms. "I'm Lisbeth! I've watched for you every single day."

The little girl with rosy cheeks crowded in. "I've watched, too! I'm Anna!"

Everyone was hugging. Aunt Inger tried to get all the children into her arms at the same time. Papa and Uncle Olav pounded each other's shoulders. Uncle Olav grabbed Lars, then lifted Peter off his feet. Mama cried. Aunt Inger cried. Then they started hugging all over again.

Uncle Olav said, "Come see the barn!"

"No, you don't!" Aunt Inger said. Her smiling

"Hello! Hello!
It's you! At last!"

46

face was flushed and red. "First we'll have supper. They're tired and hungry, Olav! They've come halfway around the world to get here."

"And we walked all day long!" Peter added.

Aunt Inger hugged Peter again. Then she turned to Mama and Papa. "You can get settled in your cabin after supper," she said. "And *tomorrow* you men can look at the barn while we women talk. Now come in and eat!"

From the doorway, Kirsten saw fresh bread and butter, a big bowl of potatoes and onions, and a platter of fresh fish on Aunt Inger's long wooden table. Her mouth watered when she noticed a berry tart cooling on the back of the stove.

"Don't worry about a little mud," Aunt Inger said as they began taking off their boots. Then she saw that their clothes were wet, too. "But look how you're soaked through!" she added. "You'll catch cold. We'll find you all some dry things right now." She bustled to a painted trunk like the one Kirsten's family had left in Riverton. From the trunk she took men's brown trousers and white shirts, a blue cotton dress for Mama, and another one for Kirsten.

"This was Lisbeth's, but she's outgrown it. It will do for now," Aunt Inger said. "Go put it on and come right down for supper."

Kirsten followed Lisbeth and Anna up the ladder to their place in the loft. Anna gave her a piece of worn quilt to dry her wet arms and legs. "Tomorrow we'll show you our secret fort," she said. "Lisbeth and I play there with our dolls."

"We'll tell you all about it later," Lisbeth added as she handed Kirsten a petticoat. "But let's hurry now. We're hungry, and I bet you are, too."

The dress from Aunt Inger was patterned with little red flowers. Kirsten pulled the soft cotton over her head and Lisbeth did up the buttons. Now Kirsten was dressed just like her cousins. She followed them down the ladder into the cozy kitchen.

When Aunt Inger saw Kirsten, she laughed and pretended to be surprised. "Who's this new girl?" she asked. "Have I met her before?"

Mama took Kirsten's hand and turned her around for a good look. "Why, don't you recognize Kirsten Larson, my American daughter?"

The next morning, Kirsten woke up in her very own bed in a small log cabin on Uncle Olav's farm. The cabin was made of split logs. It had a bare plank floor, a small fireplace, and one tiny window. Through the window, Kirsten could see a maple tree. *I'm home,* she thought. *My cousins live right next door. We'll be friends.*

The morning sun was already hot and grass-hoppers jumped in the long grass when Lisbeth and Anna led Kirsten down the path toward the stream. "You didn't tell your brothers about our fort, did you?" Anna asked. "Our fort is only for girls!"

Anna's cheerful, round face made Kirsten smile. "No, Anna, I didn't tell them about the fort. I can keep a secret, I promise," she said.

"Oh, good!" Anna carried her rag doll under her arm. The doll's smiling, painted face made Kirsten miss Sari all over again.

Lisbeth held up her hand for them to stop walking. "Is anyone coming?" she asked Anna.

Anna scampered back a few steps and looked down the path they followed through the woods.

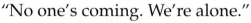

"No one's coming. We're alone."

"Follow me, then," Lisbeth told Kirsten. She lifted up a pine branch and stepped off the trail into the woods. A carpet of sweet-smelling pine needles covered the ground under the trees.

"We go to our fort through the pines so we won't leave footprints," Anna explained. "We don't want anyone to know where we are."

"Here's the entrance," Lisbeth said. She went down on her knees and crawled into a tunnel made by sumac branches. Kirsten tucked up the skirt of her new dress and crawled after her.

The tunnel ended under the green branches of a wild cherry tree. Lisbeth sat back on her heels. "Here's our fort, Kirsten."

Anna pulled off her sunbonnet and hung it from a branch. "Do you like it here?" she asked.

Kirsten looked around. The overhanging branches made a small, cool room under the tree. She let out a long breath. "Oh, yes!" she said.

"Here's where our dolls sleep," Lisbeth said. She laid her doll on a bed

made of sticks tied together at the
corners with braided grass. "Now, come
up to the loft. Hold tightly so you don't
fall." She grabbed the lowest limb of the tree and
pulled herself up into the branches. Kirsten gave
Anna a boost up, then climbed after her onto a
strong limb.

"Here's where we keep a lookout for boys,"
Anna said, swinging her legs. "Of course we've
never seen a boy in the woods, but with Lars and
Peter here, we might."

"If we see a boy, we'll get down low and stay
quiet," Lisbeth said. "That's one of our rules, Kirsten.
Do you promise to keep the rules?"

"I promise to keep all your rules," Kirsten
said. She looked out over the trees. When she left
Sweden she never imagined she was on her way
to a hiding place in a cherry tree.

"Since you live here now, you must have a place
in our fort just for your doll," Lisbeth said.

"Choose where!" Anna insisted.

Kirsten peered down through the
branches into the fort below. "There,"
Kirsten said, and she pointed to a

*"Since you live here now, you
must have a place in our fort," Lisbeth said.*

moss-covered spot. She scooted down the tree and patted the moss. It was soft and cool. Oh, Sari would like it here!

Anna climbed down, too. She got her doll and walked her across the fort to Sari's spot. "I'm coming to visit," she made her doll say. "Where is Sari?"

"Sari's still on her way," Kirsten answered. "But come visit me! *I'm* here!"

LOOKING BACK

AMERICA
IN
1854

When Kirsten's family came to America, they fit all of their belongings into two big trunks. If your family decided to move to another country, could you do that? How would you know what to bring with you? What would you leave behind? One of your relatives probably had to make decisions like these,

Immigrants used baskets and blankets to carry their belongings.

because there is a story like Kirsten's in nearly every American family. Most people who live in the United States today had relatives who were *immigrants*—people who left their home country and moved to America to start a new life. They may have settled here more than a hundred years ago, or they may have come more recently. Immigrants still come to the United States today.

Many of the early immigrants came from countries where farmland was poor. People were starving because they could not grow enough food. Like Kirsten and her family, they came to America because they wanted new land and a chance for a better life.

Immigrants who had already come to America wrote letters back home to their neighbors and relatives, telling them that life in America was good. "The land is rich," they wrote. "The grass is so thick that in one day we can cut enough to feed a cow for a whole winter." They encouraged others to join them on the frontier, in places like Minnesota, where there was plenty of good land for anyone who was willing to work hard.

People who decided to go to America could bring only their most important things with them. They filled their big trunks with clothes, blankets, tools, and food for the trip. They also packed things that would remind them of the people they loved and the places they left behind. A woman like Mama might have made room for

A Swedish family reads a letter from relatives in America.

beautiful cloth that her mother had woven, or for a
bowl that her father had carved, or for the wooden
molds she always used to decorate butter or cheese.
What do you think a girl like Kirsten might have
squeezed in?

When their trunks were finally packed, a family
had to travel to a port city and wait until a ship like

the *Eagle* was ready to sail for
America. These ships were
filled with cargo such as lumber
and iron, so there was only a small
space on them for people.

Immigrants traveled in a lower part of the ship
called *steerage*. People in steerage were cramped and
uncomfortable. The ceiling was so low that a man
couldn't stand up straight. There were no windows
for light or fresh air. There were no bathrooms, and it
was hard to get clean water for drinking or washing.
Families slept on narrow wooden bunks that were
covered with straw. Often two or more people shared
a bunk that was smaller than your bed is.

Usually a mother cooked her family's meal on the
ship's deck. At the
beginning of the
voyage, a family's
food was fresh.
But there were no
refrigerators in
1854, so the food
soon spoiled.
Before the passen-
gers reached land,
even their salted
meat was rotten

*Even in rough weather, passengers spent their time
on deck, where the air was fresh.*

and their bread was moldy. Still, they ate this food because it was all they had.

When Kirsten came to America, a very fast ship could sail across the ocean in six weeks. If the wind was bad, the trip would take much longer. Sometimes immigrants died in storms and shipwrecks on the way to America. And even with good weather, many passengers got seasick. Some of them got terrible diseases, such as cholera.

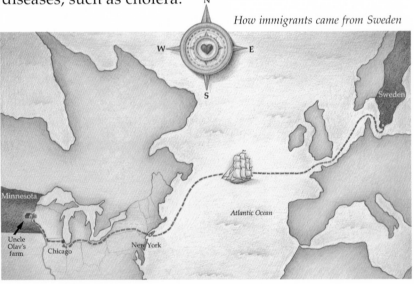

How immigrants came from Sweden

Once an immigrant family arrived safely in America, the dangers of the trip were not over. Most immigrants could not speak English, and they did not have anyone to help them buy fresh food or train tickets for their trip to the frontier. Sometimes thieves robbed or cheated the immigrants.

Immigrants arriving in America

Immigrating to America in 1854 was certainly dangerous, but it was exciting, too. If Kirsten's family had stayed in Sweden, she would probably never have seen the ocean or even a town more than 20 miles from the place she was born. Because they became immigrants, she traveled halfway around the world. She saw machines she had never dreamed of, like trains and paddle-wheel boats. She saw busy cities like New York and Chicago. She saw long stretches of open prairie and miles of rich farmland. And at the end of her journey, she had a new home in a new land, with a life full of opportunity ahead of her.

A SNEAK PEEK AT

Kirsten
LEARNS A LESSON

*Kirsten leaves secret gifts for a mysterious
Indian girl. Can she and the girl become friends?*

he next morning, when Kirsten went down to the stream to fetch Mama a bucket of water, a V of geese was flying south. She stopped on the path to watch the geese. Then she stopped again when she came upon a deer drinking at the stream.

She stood very still and waited for the deer to finish drinking. Then she looked across the stream. Turtles sunned on a fallen log. A frog jumped into the water. Then, among the cattails, she saw a dark face watching her—dark eyes, black hair, the fringed sleeve of a deerskin dress. An Indian girl stood right there!

Kirsten held her breath. The Indian girl looked at her without blinking.

"Hello," Kirsten said softly.

The Indian girl didn't speak or move. But the word startled the deer away into the pines. When Kirsten looked back from the deer for the Indian girl, she was gone.

Kirsten thought maybe she'd only imagined the girl had been there. Maybe her eyes had played tricks on her. She crossed the stream on the stones and walked a little way into the cattails. No one. But when she went back to the shore, she saw there was a footprint in the soft sand. And near the footprint was a blue bead no larger than a gooseberry. The girl must have dropped it.

Kirsten stooped and picked up the bead. She wrapped it in her hankie and put it deep into her apron pocket. As she filled her bucket with water, Kirsten wondered if the girl had been sent here for water, too. Kirsten wanted to meet her. How could she do that? Would the girl come again?

Kirsten had an idea. She set down her bucket, hurried into the woods, and crawled into the fort. She took one of the doll cakes decorated with a circle of tiny snail shells. Then she crossed the stream again and laid the doll cake on the sand by the girl's footprints. If the Indian girl came back to the stream, maybe she'd find the doll cake. If she did, she'd know it was Kirsten who left it there.

When Kirsten got back to the cabin, her breakfast waited for her on the table. Mama scolded, "You were gone so long I thought you'd lost your way. Lars and Peter have already left for school. Hurry, or you'll be late."

All day Kirsten wondered about the Indian

65

girl. When Kirsten went back to the stream after supper, the doll cake was gone. In its place was the

green wing feather of a duck, stuck into the sand like a little flag. Kirsten smiled as she picked up the duck feather and put it into her hankie with the bead.

Maybe there was a way to make friends with the dark-eyed girl.

Every morning and every evening when she went for water, Kirsten looked for the Indian girl. Kirsten didn't know exactly when the girl came to the stream, but she knew when she'd been there. Because every time Kirsten left a gift on the shore, the girl took it and left something in its place.

Once Kirsten left a piece of red yarn wrapped around a white pebble. In its place she found a length of leather thong as smooth as silk.

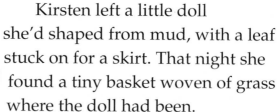

Kirsten left a little doll she'd shaped from mud, with a leaf stuck on for a skirt. That night she found a tiny basket woven of grass where the doll had been.

Kirsten left a green button on a

loop of green thread. It was replaced by
a purple bead.

Kirsten strung the two beads on the
leather thong. She kept them wrapped in
her hankie with the feather and the tiny basket.
These were her secret treasures, and the Indian girl
was her secret friend. At school, when Kirsten was
tired of writing and numbers, of trying to please
Miss Winston, she daydreamed of running off across
the prairie with the Indian girl. They wouldn't need
to talk. They'd run faster than the wind.

How Kirsten wanted to see the mysterious girl
again! One evening she saved her slice of bread and
honey from supper. She wrapped the honey sandwich
in oak leaves. Then she went to the stream for water.
She put the package of oak leaves on the other shore,
then settled down to wait. Maybe the Indian girl
came here at dusk. Kirsten decided she would meet
her, no matter what.

But the sun was almost down. Kirsten wasn't
allowed to stay away from the cabin after sunset—
Mama would worry. "Please come," Kirsten
whispered under her breath, as though that would
make the Indian girl appear.

And then, there she was! In her dress of soft deerskin, the Indian girl slipped silently through the cattails. She stooped and picked up the oak leaf package. She peeled off the leaves, sniffed, and began to eat the bread and honey. As she ate she looked right at Kirsten. Kirsten didn't speak. She didn't want to frighten the girl away again. Instead, she walked slowly forward, watching the girl.

The girl was a little smaller than Kirsten. Her hair and skin shone as if they'd been polished. Kirsten thought she'd never seen eyes so inky black. The Indian girl licked honey from her finger. She watched Kirsten, too.

Dark shadows moved on the stream as Kirsten crossed the stones. When she stood in front of the Indian girl, the girl reached into the leather pouch she wore around her waist. She held out to Kirsten a tiny clay pot decorated with markings that might have been made from a sharp twig.

Kirsten took the little pot. It was as small as an acorn. "It's pretty!" she breathed.

The Indian girl looked at her hard. Slowly, as though she feared she would scare Kirsten, she reached out and touched Kirsten's yellow braid.

68

*Slowly, the Indian girl
reached out and touched Kirsten's yellow braid.*

READ ALL OF KIRSTEN'S STORIES,
available at bookstores and *www.americangirl.com.*

MEET KIRSTEN • An American Girl
Kirsten and her family make the difficult journey from
Sweden to begin a new life on the Minnesota frontier.

KIRSTEN LEARNS A LESSON • A School Story
Kirsten must learn English at school. She learns an
important lesson from her secret Indian friend, too.

KIRSTEN'S SURPRISE • A Christmas Story
Kirsten and Papa travel to town to get their trunks from
Sweden. Their errand turns into a terrifying trip.

HAPPY BIRTHDAY, KIRSTEN! • A Springtime Story
After taking care of Mama and the new baby, Kirsten gets
a birthday surprise during the Larsons' barn raising.

KIRSTEN SAVES THE DAY • A Summer Story
Kirsten and Peter find honey in the woods, but their
discovery leads to a dangerous adventure.

CHANGES FOR KIRSTEN • A Winter Story
A raccoon causes a disaster for the Larsons, but Kirsten
and Lars find a treasure that means better times.

◆

WELCOME TO KIRSTEN'S WORLD • 1854
American history is lavishly illustrated
with photographs, illustrations, and
excerpts from real girls' letters and diaries.